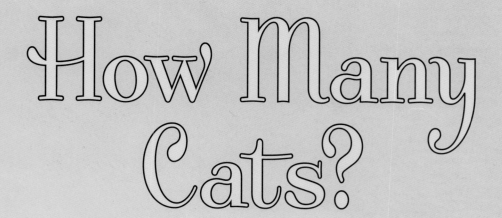

# How Many Cats?

by Lauren Thompson

*illustrated by* Robin Eley

DISNEY · HYPERION BOOKS

NEW YORK

Please note: Yarn can be dangerous for cats.
The cats in this book play safely with yarn, but please supervise your own
cats carefully when they play with yarn, string, or ribbons.

Text © 2009 by Lauren Thompson
Illustrations © 2009 by Robin Eley
All rights reserved.  Published by Disney•Hyperion Books, an imprint of Disney Book
Group. No part of this book may be reproduced or transmitted in any form or by any
means, electronic or mechanical, including photocopying, recording, or by any information
storage and retrieval system, without written permission from the publisher.
For information address Disney•Hyperion Books,
114 Fifth Avenue, New York, New York 10011-5690.
First Edition
10 9 8 7 6 5 4 3 2 1
Printed in Singapore
Reinforced binding
ISBN 978-1-4231-0801-6
Library of Congress Cataloging-in-Publication Data on file.
Visit www.hyperionbooksforchildren.com

For Mitsie (and Sophia, Ranger,
Tiger…and Butch)
—L.T.

For Madeline, Amelia, Harrison,
Mitchell, and Liam
—R.E.

Ⓗow many cats
are here to play?
**Zero**, zilch.
None today.

Wait!
Who's that slinking home at last?
**One** clever cat, bold and fast.

One furry friend
follows behind.
How many cats?
**Two** cats—that's fine.

Now how many cats?
Just a few.
**Three** cats in all—one plus two.

Another cat slips through the door.
How many cats?
Now there are **four**.

Here's one more to lend a hand.
How many now?
**Five** cats. That's grand!

More cats arrive to join the five.
**Six**, **seven**, **eight**, **nine** cats
— divine!

Then one more kitty scampers in.
How many cats?
Count them: **ten**!

Still more friends come
one by one,
adding to the feline fun.

Eleven, twelve,
the crowd keeps growing.
Thirteen, fourteen,
overflowing!

**Fifteen, sixteen,**
skipping, scamping!
**Seventeen, eighteen,**
verving, vamping!

Then with a cheer,
two more playful pals appear.
How many cats in all? Plenty!
Now they number **nineteen**, **twenty**.

Twenty cats jump and jive,
frolicking in four rows of five.

Then five tired cats leave the scene.
How many cats are left?

**Fifteen**.
Fifteen kitties sprint and spree,
in five galloping groups of three.

Three cats take off down the hall.
How many left?

Just **twelve**, that's all.

Twelve fine cats in three lines of four

flaunt and flounce across the floor.

Four cats make a grand escape.
How many cats are left?

**Eight**.
Eight cats leapfrog across the room,
two by two by two by two.

Two cats exit side by side.

Now just **six** are
left inside.

Six cats caper happily,
prowling 'round in two troops of three.

One cat trio takes a bow.
How many left?
Just **three** cats now.

Three cats skip across the floor,
then—zip!—skedaddle out the door.

Now how many cats?
The sum is where it had begun.
**Zero**, null,
nada, none.

Zero cats?
What fun is that?

Count them again,
cat by cat!